For my old friend, Bill Vickery,
and for Jim, who knows the magic

J. L.

For Andy and Pete,
Mannerheim and Schmetz

A. G.

First published 2001 by Walker Books Ltd
87 Vauxhall Walk, London SE11 5HJ

2 4 6 8 10 9 7 5 3 1

Text © 2001 Jonathan London
Illustrations © 2001 Adam Gustavson

This book has been typeset in Journal Text

Printed in Hong Kong

British Library Cataloguing in Publication Data:
a catalogue record for this book is
available from the British Library

ISBN 0-7445-7304-1

Where the Big Fish Are

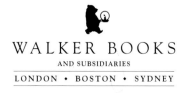

Written by Jonathan London · Illustrated by Adam Gustavson

WALKER BOOKS
AND SUBSIDIARIES
LONDON · BOSTON · SYDNEY

All summer we talk about it – about going out to where the really big fish are. Then one day, tired of saying, "If we had a raft..."

I jump up and say, "Let's go!"

We race back up the slope behind the jetty.
I can hear Bill huffing behind me.
"Used to be tracks round here," I yell.

"Wait up, will yer!" Bill pants.

"Railway tracks," I say.

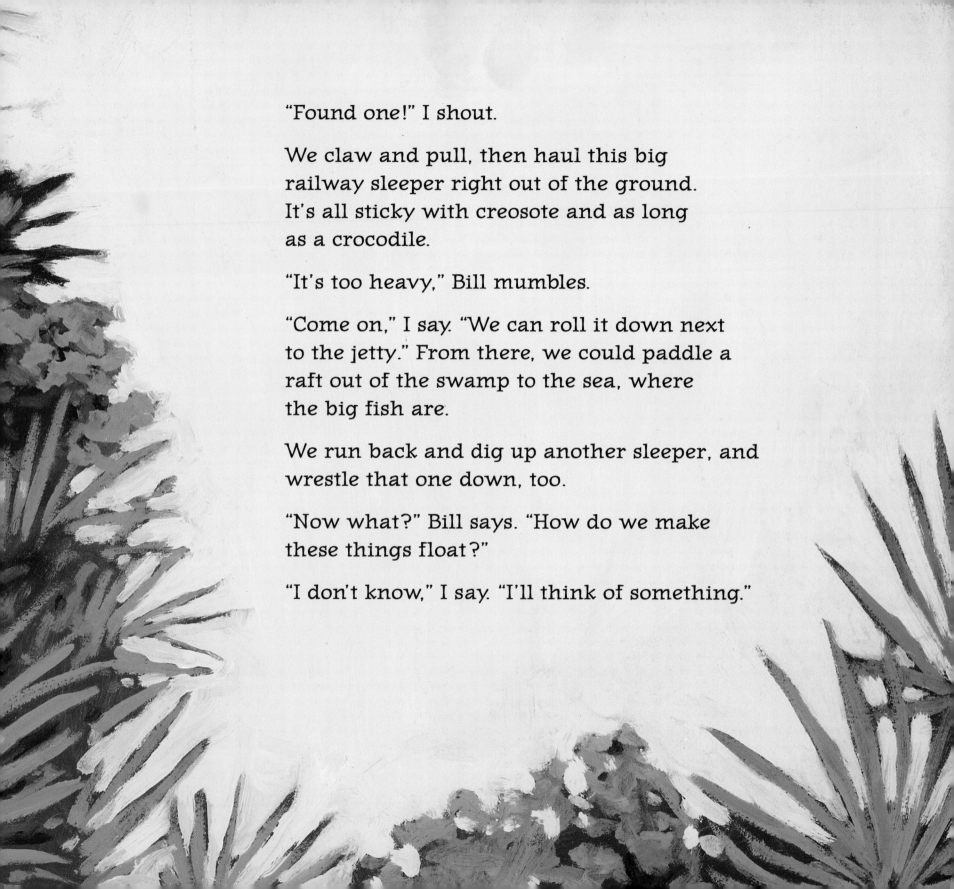

"Found one!" I shout.

We claw and pull, then haul this big
railway sleeper right out of the ground.
It's all sticky with creosote and as long
as a crocodile.

"It's too heavy," Bill mumbles.

"Come on," I say. "We can roll it down next
to the jetty." From there, we could paddle a
raft out of the swamp to the sea, where
the big fish are.

We run back and dig up another sleeper, and
wrestle that one down, too.

"Now what?" Bill says. "How do we make
these things float?"

"I don't know," I say. "I'll think of something."

At supper, I make
a raft on my plate
with fish fingers
and chips.
"Stop playing
with your food!"
Mum says.

Then she brings
out doughnuts
for dessert.

The next morning,
I sprint to Bill's
house.

"Wake up!
Wake up!"

He grumbles
and groans.

"Inner tubes,"
I whisper.

"What...?
What...?"

"Inner tubes!"

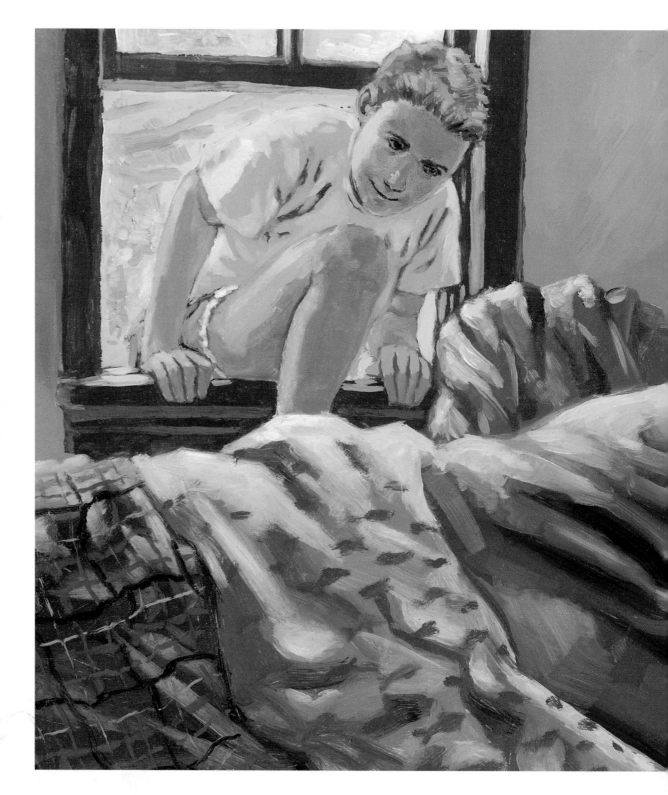

For a handful of change, the scrapyard man lets us have two huge inner tubes. They're full of holes, but we patch them up – and roll them along like giant black doughnuts.

Back at the jetty, Bill lashes the inner tubes between the sleepers with rope. I nail some old warped planks across the top.

Bill sweats like mad – and gets a splinter in his thumb – "Ouch!" He's just about ready to give up, but when I start talking about fishing, he starts wrestling with that rope again.

When we're done, Bill finds an old flagpole. "Think this will work as a mast?" he asks. We rig it up, then shove the raft into the water and tie it to the jetty.

"Hey, it floats!" Bill shouts. He's so excited he does a little dance.

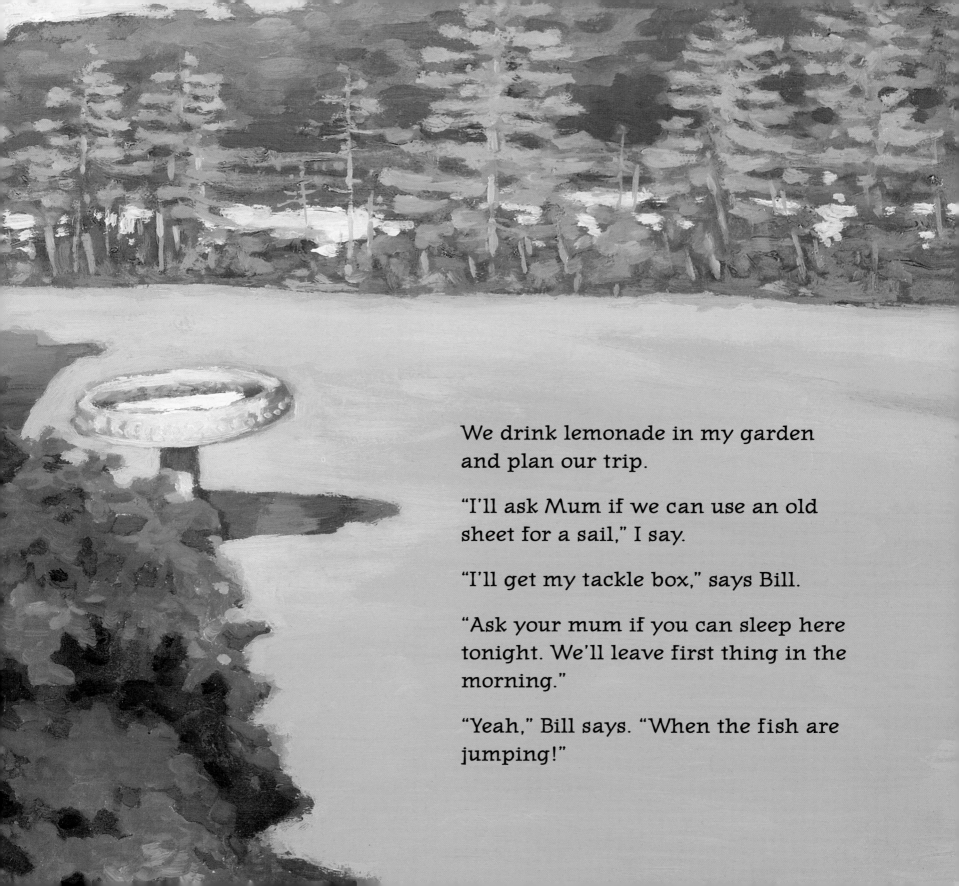

We drink lemonade in my garden and plan our trip.

"I'll ask Mum if we can use an old sheet for a sail," I say.

"I'll get my tackle box," says Bill.

"Ask your mum if you can sleep here tonight. We'll leave first thing in the morning."

"Yeah," Bill says. "When the fish are jumping!"

The first drops hit
the windows around
midnight, hard as
pebbles. It's like
a hurricane outside.
The wind slams like a
sledgehammer into
the house.

I look over at Bill's
sleeping bag.
He's gone.

The raft! I think,
and race outside.

Down in the swamp I see the raft crashing
around at the end of the jetty.
And there's Bill, hanging on to the rope
like he's hauling in a huge fish.

"Bill!" I shout.

Just as I get to him,
the rope snaps – but
Bill hangs on – and
I do a flying tackle.
The rope whips loose
from his hands, and
the raft disappears
into the storm.

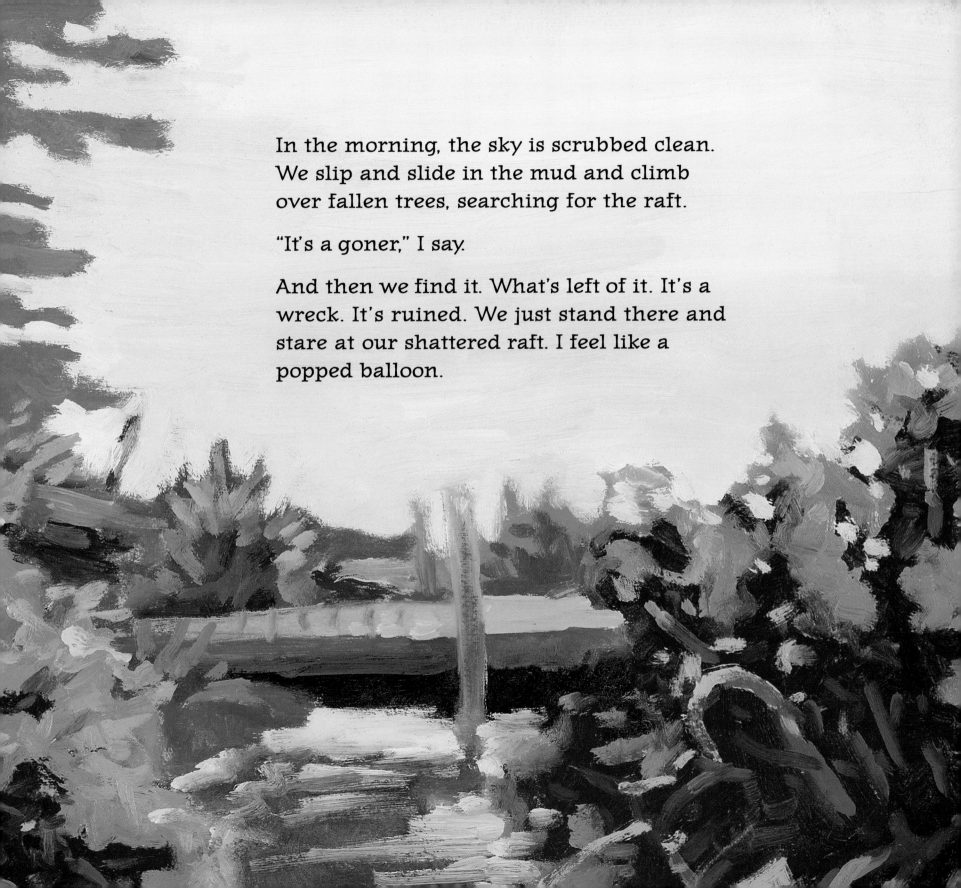

In the morning, the sky is scrubbed clean.
We slip and slide in the mud and climb
over fallen trees, searching for the raft.

"It's a goner," I say.

And then we find it. What's left of it. It's a
wreck. It's ruined. We just stand there and
stare at our shattered raft. I feel like a
popped balloon.

But Bill, he's like a turtle, slow but sure.
He turns to me and says, "Better get our
hammers." I look at him like he's crazy.
"Those fish are waiting!" he says.

Then we get to work. We pick up the best of
the busted planks, straighten bent and twisted
nails and fix everything the storm has broken.

When we're done, we push our raft back into
the water and grab our things and hop aboard.
It tips. We almost fall … then catch our balance.

"Let's go fishing!" Bill shouts.

Then slowly we paddle our way out
to sea, where the big fish are.

"I bet I catch the biggest fish," I say.
But I'm just joking. I bet Bill catches
the biggest one today.